nickelodeon

Pups Sa
Pool Day

Parragon

Bath • New York • Cologne • Melbourne • Delhi
Hong Kong • Shenzhen • Singapore

It's a hot and sunny day in Adventure Bay. Rocky and Rubble are in the park.

"I need to cool down," says Rubble. "Let's take a dip in the pool!"

Rocky and Rubble head to the pool, but when they get there, it's empty!

"Oh, no! What happened to the water?" says Rocky.

"I don't know, but we have to find out. This is a job for the PAW Patrol!" says Rubble. "Let's go."

Over at the Lookout, Skye and Marshall are packing things for a day at the pool.

"Are you ready?" says Skye.

"Almost," calls Marshall. "I just need my towel, sun cream, hat, water, and my Super Dog comic book. Now I'm ready!"

Rubble and Rocky race down Main Street to find Ryder.

"Hey, pups," says Ryder. "What's wrong?"

"There's no water in the pool," pants Rocky.

"No water? What are we going to do?" asks Alex.

"Don't worry, Alex," says Ryder, pulling out his Pup Pad. "The PAW Patrol will fix it." He hits the alarm button and calls the pups to the Lookout.

The pups line up in the control room.

"The water from the water tower isn't reaching the pool," says Ryder. "We need to find out why."

"Marshall, I need your ladder to check out the tower. And Rubble, I need your shovel in case we need to dig up a blocked pipe."

The pups are excited to help.

"Everyone else, head to the pool!" says Ryder.

Ryder, Rubble and Marshall arrive at the water tower. The pad holding up the tower has slipped, and the water pipe is bent.

"We have to fix the tower before we can fix the pipe," says Ryder. "We just need a few more paws to help us!"

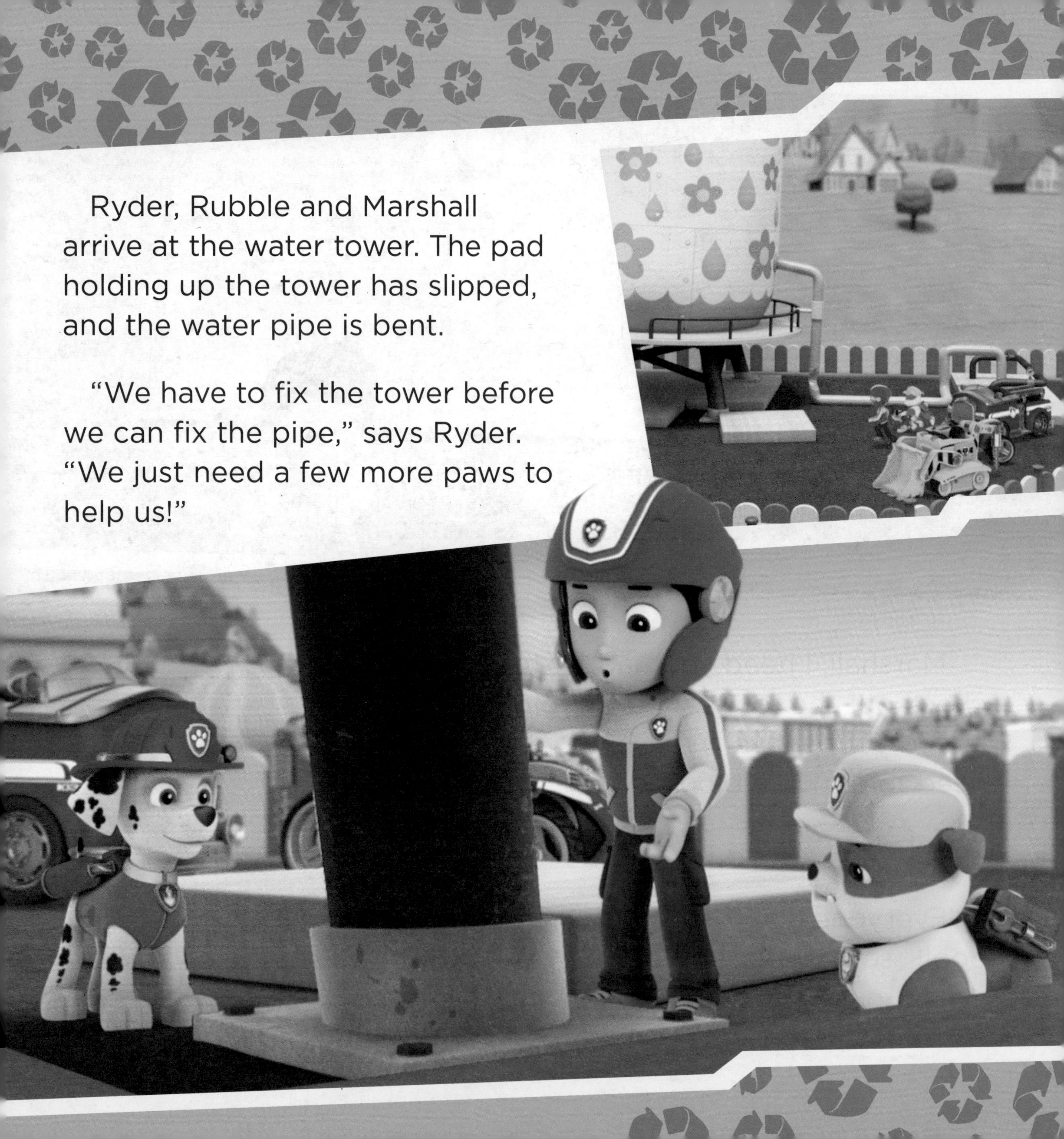

Ryder calls Rocky and Chase. "Chase, we need your winch. Rocky, we need your forklift, too."

"You got it, Ryder!" bark Chase and Rocky.

When Rocky and Chase arrive at the water tower, all the pups leap into action.

"OK, PAW Patrol, you each have an important job to do!" says Ryder.

"Chase, can we use your cable hook and winch motor?"

"On the way!" says Chase.

"Marshall," calls Ryder. "Can you climb up and attach the hook to the tower?"

"Winch cable is hooked on!" says Marshall.

Next, Rubble uses his digger to make a pile of earth near the tower.

"Great job, Rubble," says Ryder. "Now Rocky, use your forklift to pick up the cement pad, so Rubble can put the earth underneath."

"Let's do it!" says Rocky.

Meanwhile at the pool, Skye has an idea to keep everyone cool. She flies right to the top of Jake's mountain.

"What could be cooler than snow?" says Skye.

"Check it out," says Zuma. "Here comes Skye to cool us off!"

But when Skye drops the snow, it all lands on Zuma!
"First I was a hot dog, now I'm an ice pup!" says Zuma.

Back at the water tower, the PAW Patrol are finishing the repairs.

Chase pulls the tower with his winch. Rocky lifts the cement pad and Rubble dumps earth under it.

"Cement pad, going back down," calls Rocky. When it's in place, Chase releases the winch. The water tower straightens out.

"Great!" says Ryder. "Now let's fix the bent pipe and get the water flowing again."

Rocky finds a spare pipe in his recycling truck and screws it into place.

"That should do it!" says Rocky. "Let's see if we fixed it."

Ryder calls Skye on the Pup Pad. “Skye, I’m just about to turn the water back on! The pool should start filling up any second now.”

“Thanks, Ryder,” says Skye. “Get ready everyone, the water is on its way!”

Everyone waits by the pool, then suddenly a huge jet of water bursts out. Pool day is saved!

"Hooray!" they all cheer.

When the pool has completely filled up, Zuma says, “All right, everybody. Ready, set… get wet!

Ryder and the other pups arrive at the pool.

"Thanks for fixing the pool, PAW Patrol!" says Alex.

"You're welcome, Alex," says Ryder. "Remember, whenever there's trouble, just yelp for help!"